Marvin's Manners

Written by Anne Myers
Illustrated by Esther Szegedy

STECK-VAUGHN
ELEMENTARY · SECONDARY · ADULT · LIBRARY

A Harcourt Classroom Education Company

www.steck-vaughn.com

Marvin came over to play.

Marvin did not share.

Marvin did not take turns.

Marvin did not clean up.

Marvin did not have any manners!

I helped Marvin.

Now Marvin is cool!